KIDS' TRAVEL GUIDE

UK & LONDON

FlyingKids PRESENTS:

KIDS' TRAVEL GUIDE

UK & LONDON

Author: Sara-Jane Williams
Editor: Carma Graber
Graphic designer: Francesca Guido
Published by FlyingKids Limited

Visit us @ **www.theflyingkids.com**
Contact us: **leonardo@theflyingkids.com**

ISBN: 978-1910994115

Table of Contents

Dear Parents,

If you bought this book, you're probably planning a family trip with your kids. You are spending a lot of time and money in the hopes that this family vacation will be pleasant and fun. Of course, you would like your **children** to get to know the place you are visiting—a little of its geography, local **history**, important sites, **culture**, customs, and more. And you hope they will always remember the trip as a very special **experience**.

The reality is often quite different. Parents find themselves **frustrated** as they struggle to convince their kids to join a tour or visit a landmark, while the kids just want to stay in and watch TV. Or the kids are glued to their mobile devices and don't pay much attention to the new sights and places of interest. Many parents are **disappointed** when they return home and discover that their kids **don't remember** much about the trip and the new things they learned. That's exactly why the Kids' Travel Guide series was created.

With the Kids' Travel Guides, young children become **researchers** and **active participants** in the trip. During the vacation, kids will read relevant facts about the place you are visiting, and they'll find **puzzles**, **tasks** to complete, useful **tips**, and other recommendations along the way.

The kids will meet **Leonardo—their tour guide**. Leonardo encourages them to experiment, explore, and be more **involved in the family's activities**—as well as to learn new information and make memories throughout the trip. In addition, kids are encouraged to document and write about their experiences during the trip, so that when you return home, they will have a memoir that will be fun to look at and reread again and again. The Kids' Travel Guides support children as they **get ready** for the trip, **visit** new places, **learn** new things, and finally, return **home**.

The *Kids' Travel Guide – UK & London* focuses on the **United Kingdom** and **London**—also known as **"The Smoke."** In it, children will learn about **the United Kingdom**—its geography, history, unique culture, traditions, and more—along with **background information** on **London** and its special attractions. The **London** portion of the book concentrates on **central sites** that are recommended for children. At each of these sites, interesting facts, **action items**, and **quizzes** await your kids. You, the parents, are invited to participate, or to find an available bench and relax while you enjoy your **active** children.

If you are reading this book, it means you are lucky—you are going to **London, in the United Kingdom**!

You may have noticed that your parents are getting ready for the journey. They have bought travel guides, looked for information on the Internet, and printed pages of information. They are talking to friends and people who have already visited the United Kingdom and London, in order to learn about it and know what to do, where to go, and when ...

But this book is not just another guidebook for your parents.
This book is for you only—the young traveler.

So what is this book all about?

First and foremost, meet Leonardo, your very own personal guide on this trip. Leonardo has visited many places around the world. (Guess how he got there? 🙂)
He will be with you throughout the book and the trip. Leonardo will tell you all about the places you will visit—it is always good to learn a little bit about the city and its history beforehand.
Leonardo will provide many ideas, quizzes, tips, and other surprises.
He will be with you while you are packing and leaving home, and he will stay in the hotel with you (don't worry, it does not cost more money 😉)!
And he will see the sights with you until you return home. 🙂

HAVE FUN!

A TRAVEL DIARY — THE BEGINNING!

GOING TO LONDON, UK!!!

How did you get to London?

By plane / ship / car / other ____________

We will stay in London for______days.

Is this your first visit ? ____________

Where will you sleep? In a hotel / in a campsite / in a motel / in an apartment / with family / in a guesthouse / other ____________

What places are you planning to visit?

____

____

____

____

What special activities are you planning to do?

____

____

____

____

Who is traveling?

Write down the names of family members traveling with you and their answers to the questions.

Name: ______

Age: ______

Has he or she visited the UK or London before? yes / no

What is the most exciting thing about your upcoming trip?

______

______

______

Name: ______

Age: ______

Has he or she visited the UK or London before? yes / no

What is the most exciting thing about your upcoming trip?

______

______

______

Name: ______

Age: ______

Has he or she visited the UK or London before? yes / no

What is the most exciting thing about your upcoming trip?

______

______

______

Name: ______

Age: ______

Has he or she visited the UK or London before? yes / no

What is the most exciting thing about your upcoming trip?

______

______

______

Name: ______

Age: ______

Has he or she visited the UK or London before? yes / no

What is the most exciting thing about your upcoming trip?

______

______

______

Paste a picture of your family.

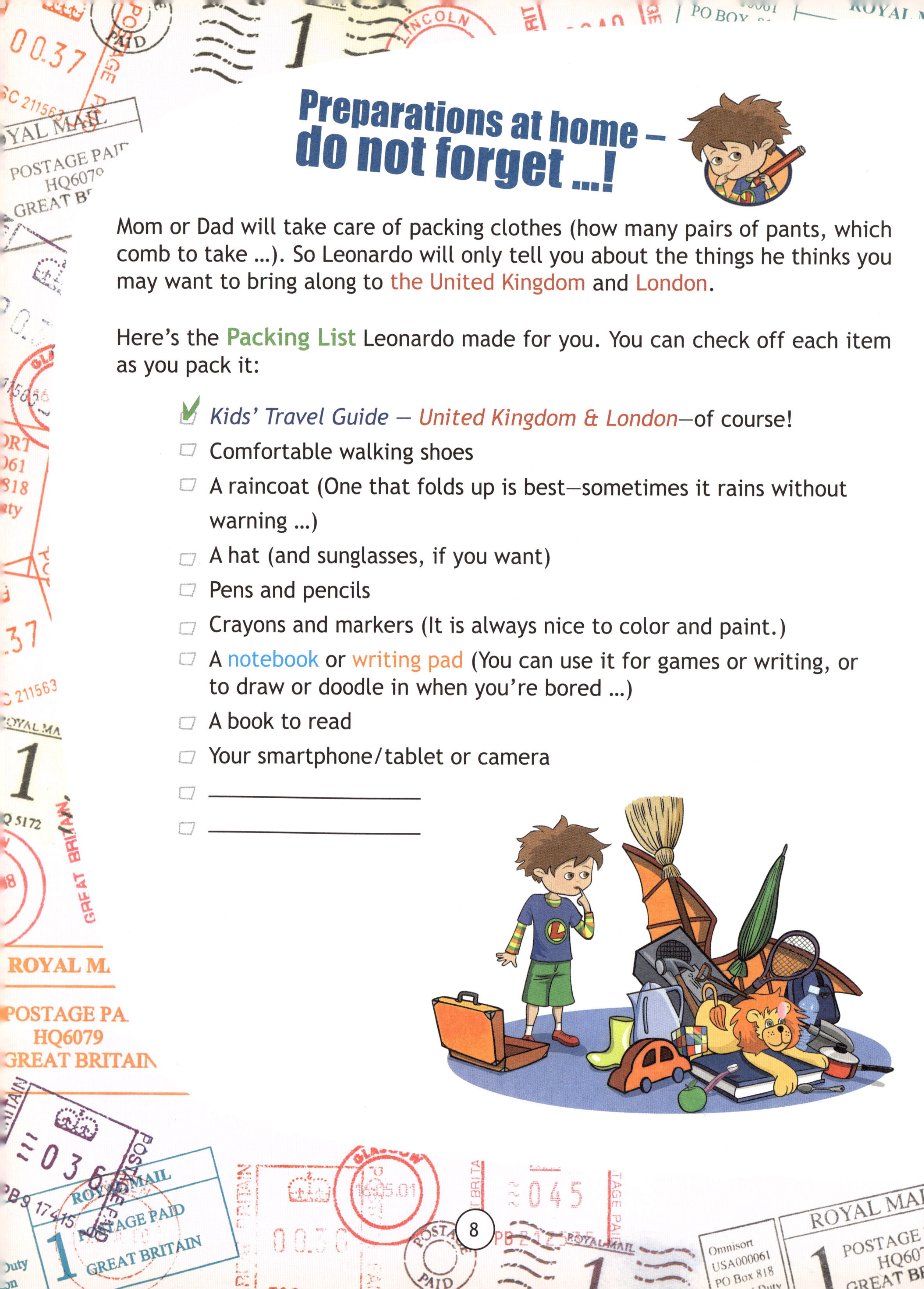

Preparations at home – do not forget ...!

Mom or Dad will take care of packing clothes (how many pairs of pants, which comb to take ...). So Leonardo will only tell you about the things he thinks you may want to bring along to the United Kingdom and London.

Here's the Packing List Leonardo made for you. You can check off each item as you pack it:

- ☑ *Kids' Travel Guide – United Kingdom & London*—of course!
- ☐ Comfortable walking shoes
- ☐ A raincoat (One that folds up is best—sometimes it rains without warning ...)
- ☐ A hat (and sunglasses, if you want)
- ☐ Pens and pencils
- ☐ Crayons and markers (It is always nice to color and paint.)
- ☐ A notebook or writing pad (You can use it for games or writing, or to draw or doodle in when you're bored ...)
- ☐ A book to read
- ☐ Your smartphone/tablet or camera
- ☐ ____________________
- ☐ ____________________

TIPS!

Pack your things in a small bag (or backpack). You may also want to take these things:

- Snacks, fruit, candy, and chewing gum. If you are flying, it can help a lot during takeoff and landing, when there's pressure in your ears.
- Some games you can play while sitting down: electronic games, booklets of crossword puzzles, connect-the-numbers (or connect-the-dots), etc.

Now let's see if you can find 12 items you should take on a trip in this word search puzzle:

- Leonardo
- walking shoes
- hat
- raincoat
- crayons
- book
- pencil
- camera
- snacks
- fruit
- patience
- good mood

P	A	T	I	E	N	C	E	A	W	F	G
E	L	R	T	S	G	Y	J	W	A	T	O
Q	E	Y	U	Y	K	Z	K	M	L	W	O
H	O	S	N	A	S	N	Y	S	K	G	D
A	N	R	Z	C	P	E	N	C	I	L	M
C	A	M	E	R	A	A	W	G	N	E	O
R	R	A	I	N	C	O	A	T	G	Q	O
Y	D	S	G	I	R	K	Z	K	S	H	D
S	O	A	C	O	A	E	T	K	H	A	T
F	R	U	I	T	Y	Q	O	V	O	D	A
B	O	O	K	F	O	H	Z	K	E	R	T
T	K	Z	K	A	N	S	I	E	S	Y	U
O	V	I	E	S	S	N	A	C	K	S	P

GETTING TO KNOW THE UNITED KINGDOM!

The United Kingdom, or "the UK" for short, is made up of four different countries:
England
Scotland
Wales
Northern Ireland
The UK also includes many smaller islands around its coast. It is located in the northwestern part of Europe.

The UK has more than 17,000 kilometers (10,560 miles) of coastline—and plenty of pretty beaches! You'll also find beautiful mountains and forests, rolling fields, sparkling lakes, rushing rivers, exciting cities, cute villages, lots of churches, many old castles and historical spots, great shopping, and loads of things to see and do.

More than 64 million people live in the UK. And more than 28 million people visit it every year! It is the 11th biggest country in Europe, and it's a popular tourist spot.

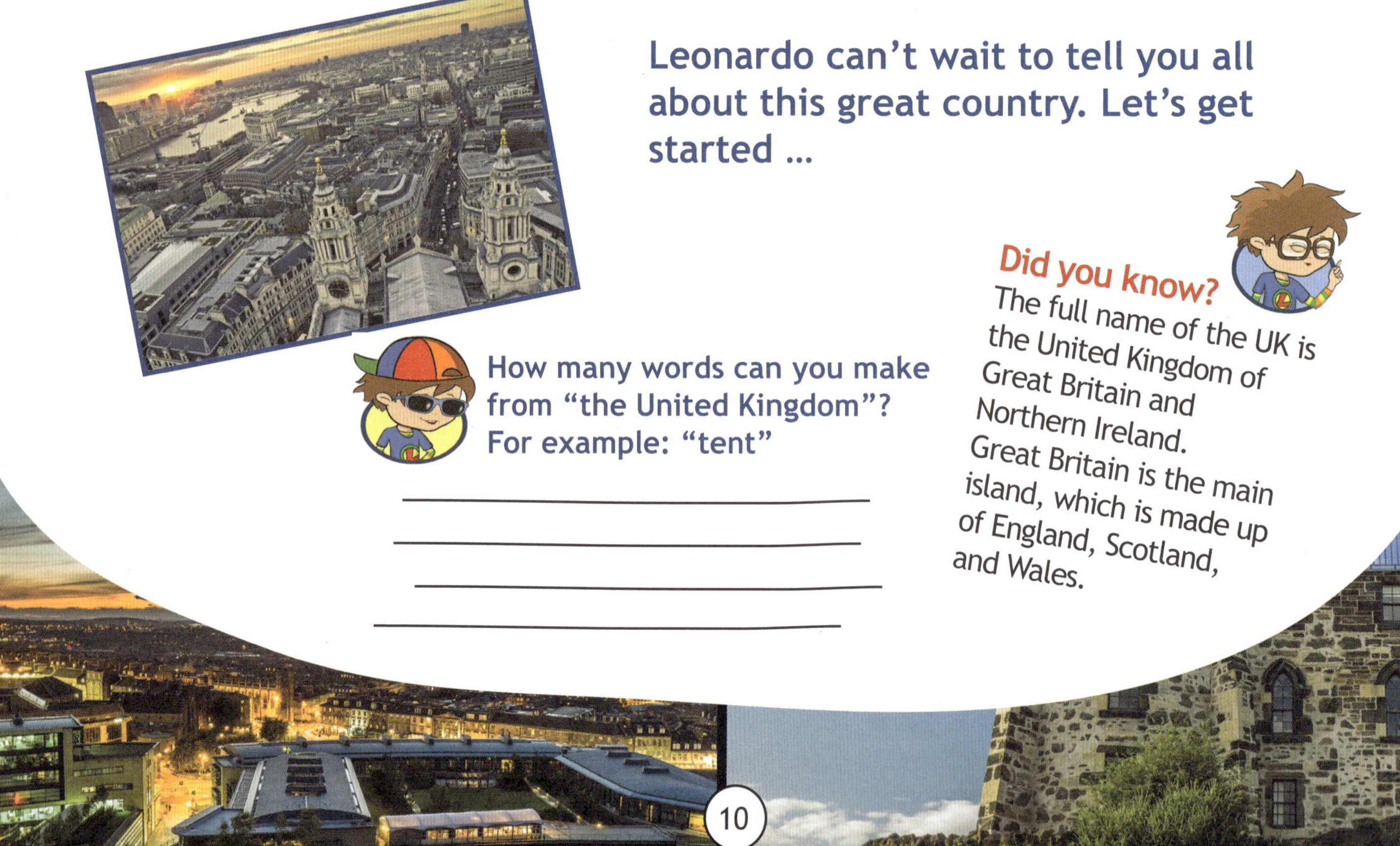

Leonardo can't wait to tell you all about this great country. Let's get started ...

How many words can you make from "the United Kingdom"? For example: "tent"

____

____

____

____

Did you know?
The full name of the UK is the United Kingdom of Great Britain and Northern Ireland. Great Britain is the main island, which is made up of England, Scotland, and Wales.

More juicy UK info!

Each country in the UK has its own special feel and traditions—and they each offer something different! They all have their own **flags** and special **saints**. And you may hear **other languages** being spoken along with English!

Leonardo wants to tell you a few things that are special about each country:

England

England is the home of the UK's capital city—London—and it's also very famous for football. The rose is a symbol of England, and Saint George is the special saint. The national tree is the oak tree, a symbol of strength and power. A famous person from English folklore was Robin Hood!

Wales

Wales is a land of dragons and castles! Many famous legends and myths come from Wales. Because of its rich countryside and successful farming, many people think of sheep when they think of Wales! The daffodil and leek are the country's national symbols, and the special saint is Saint David. You'll find the UK's smallest house in Wales!

Scotland

Scotland is very famous for kilts and bagpipes. Kilts are similar to skirts, and are worn by both women and men! Bagpipes are musical instruments that people blow into to make a very unusual sound. Traditionally, different family groups in Scottish society were called clans. Clans could be identified by their tartans (a woven cloth that has a special pattern of checks, lines, and colors for each clan).

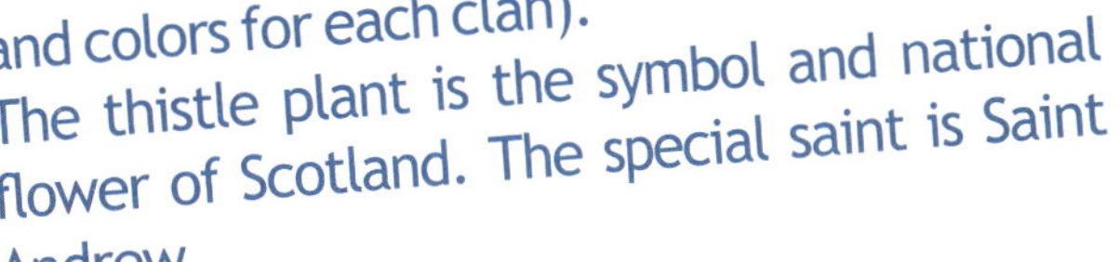

The thistle plant is the symbol and national flower of Scotland. The special saint is Saint Andrew.

Northern Ireland

Northern Ireland has not had its own national flag since 1973, but the flag with the red hand is still used unofficially. People often think of the shamrock—a three-leaved clover—when they think about Northern Ireland. The country is also famous for small people called leprechauns! Leprechauns are said to hide a pot of gold at the end of a rainbow. Saint Patrick is the special saint of Northern Ireland.

UK on the world map

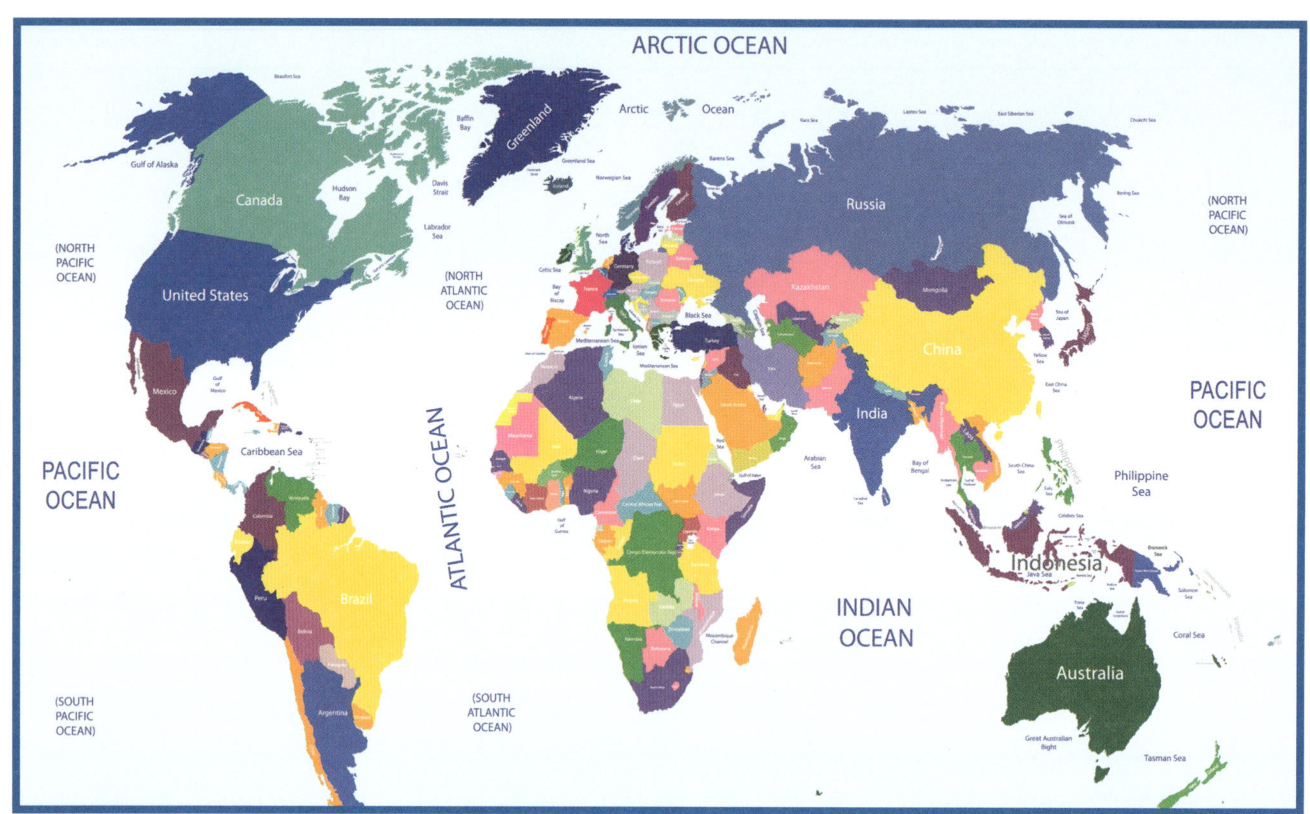

Where is the UK?

This is a map of the world. Can you help Leonardo find the UK? Mark the UK's borders. Find your home country on the map and mark its borders too.

Quizzes!

What continent is the UK on? ____________________

How many countries make up the UK? ____________________

Answers: Europe; 4 countries

What is a compass rose?

The compass rose is a drawing that shows the directions: North-South-East-West. North is always at the top of the map, and from that you can find the other directions. When you need to get to a place, you can use a compass. A compass rose is drawn on the face of the compass, and the needle always points North. This helps you to navigate and figure out what direction to go—so you can get from one place to another.

Have you ever used a compass? YES / NO

Write down the three missing directions in the blank squares:

North

North Atlantic Ocean
Scotland
North Sea
Edinburgh
Belfast
Northern Ireland
Irish Sea
Ireland
England
Wales
Cardiff
London
North Atlantic Ocean
English Channel

Can you help Leonardo with these directions?

1. What is to the north of England?

____

2. What is to the south of Northern Ireland?

____

3. What is to the east of Wales?

____

4. What sea is to the south of England?

____

5. What sea is to the east of Scotland?

____

Borders—
the lines between neighbors

Did you know?

Borders were invented to show the difference between different countries. A border is a line that marks the end of one country's land and the start of another country's land. There are many kinds of borders: Rivers and mountain ranges can be natural borders. Sometimes fences and gates are built to mark a border.
Countries sometimes end at seas, but many also have islands in the ocean.

There can also be internal borders—for example, between states, regions, counties, and provinces.

There is only one country in the UK that has a land border with two other countries. Do you know what it is? ______________________________

Help Leonardo find these 10 interesting UK cities:

- ☐ London
- ☐ Belfast
- ☐ Cardiff
- ☐ Swansea
- ☐ Edinburgh
- ☐ Glasgow
- ☐ Birmingham
- ☐ Manchester
- ☐ Liverpool
- ☐ York

L	R	E	T	S	E	H	C	N	A	M
I	O	A	L	C	I	H	A	U	H	A
S	Y	O	K	S	P	Y	R	O	G	H
W	N	W	P	D	O	R	D	C	R	G
A	A	O	X	R	M	N	I	H	U	N
N	I	G	K	E	E	E	F	G	B	I
S	B	S	Z	L	G	V	F	A	N	M
E	E	A	A	N	C	D	I	N	I	R
A	I	L	N	O	D	N	O	L	D	I
U	R	G	A	T	S	A	F	L	E	B

Each country within the UK has its own capital city—although London is the overall capital of the whole United Kingdom.

What is the capital city of your country? ______________________________

Answers: England is the only country with a land border with 2 other countries: Scotland and Wales.

Capital city—London

London is the capital of the UK, and it's also the capital of England. It is the UK's biggest city.
London's nickname is "The Smoke." You'll learn all about London—and the exciting things to see and do there—in the second part of this book.

Draw a circle around London.

Besides London, will you be visiting any other cities in the UK? If so, write their names here:

___

___

___

___

Each of the countries in the UK has its own capital city. All the cities are very different, but they all have lots of interesting places to visit and fun things to do. Leonardo wants to tell you about the capitals of Scotland, Wales, and Northern Ireland. Let's go ...

Castles and witches!
Edinburgh—the Scottish capital

Edinburgh is the **capital** of Scotland. It is the second biggest city in Scotland—and the seventh biggest in the UK. After London, it's the most popular city in the UK for tourists.

Here are Leonardo's favorite things in Edinburgh!

Edinburgh Castle

You'll see it sitting high up on a hill overlooking the rest of the city. Exploring the castle's many nooks and crannies is lots of fun! The castle is home to the Scottish Crown Jewels, known as the Honours, and some interesting old guns.

The Cadies and Witchery Tour

This is a fun-filled and spooky look at the old part of the city. Guides in wonderful costumes tell tales about witches, ghosts, and mysteries!

Holyrood Palace

This is Queen Elizabeth's official home in Scotland. It is a very grand building with beautiful rooms inside. You can see displays in the gallery that change throughout the year, and the gardens are very pretty.

Edinburgh has many museums, churches, play areas, parks, and shops to see too.

Help Leonardo find Edinburgh on the map and draw a circle around it.

Did you know?

Edinburgh's nickname is Auld Reekie. This means "Old Smoky" in English. Just like London, it got its nickname because the air was so smoky from homes heated with coal fires and the factories.

Time travel to the future and the past ... Cardiff—the Welsh capital

Cardiff is on the coast of South Wales, and it is the capital city of Wales. It was historically an industrial city, but Cardiff has been through many changes over the years ... There are now lots of modern things, and tons of things for you and your family to see and do!

Did you know?
There are five outstanding castles around Cardiff—perfect for exploring and imagining the past!

Leonardo wants to tell you about these great things to do in Cardiff:

Cardiff Castle is a 2,000-year-old castle and Roman fortress. It has huge gardens and lots of beautiful art. Llandaff Cathedral is one of the oldest religious buildings in all of Europe!

Have you ever wanted to travel through time or meet a Dalek? If so, the Doctor Who Experience will be perfect for you! And if you want to feel as if you're in the living past, go to the open-air Museum of Welsh Life! Cardiff also has great beaches!

Did you know?
Cardiff has the most park space per person of all the UK's cities. This means there are plenty of places for you to run and play!

Help Leonardo write the names of these famous Cardiff sights:

D_ _t_ r W_o E_ _ _ ri_ _ _e

C_ _ _ i_ _ C_ s_ _ _

L_ an_ _f_ C_ _ _e_ _a_

Answers: Doctor Who Experience; Cardiff Castle; Llandaff Cathedral

BANGOR
NEWTOWN
ST DAVID'S
SWANSEA
CARDIFF

Can you spot Cardiff on the map? Put a star next to it.

Dinosaurs, mummies, caves, and more ... Belfast—the Northern Irish capital

Belfast is both the capital city and the biggest city of Northern Ireland.

It was a very dangerous city in the past, with lots of fighting and violence between Northern Ireland and the Republic of Ireland. These times were known as "The Troubles."

Luckily, Belfast is now at peace—it was even given an award for being the safest city in the whole UK!

Did you know?
The famous ship *Titanic* was built in Belfast.

But what can you DO in Belfast?—LOTS!

These are some top things that Leonardo recommends:

Belfast Castle and Cave Hill

The castle itself is fairly new (compared to other castles)—it only dates back to 1870! It is more like a big and grand house. The nearby caves are incredibly cool and great for exploring!

Belfast Zoo

Do you love animals? Then Belfast Zoo will provide a fun day for you and your family! It has a splendid lake and lots of animals!

Help Leonardo by drawing a star next to Belfast on the map.

Ulster Museum

Have you ever wanted to get up close and personal with dinosaurs? Or learn more about ancient Egyptian mummies? These are just two things you can do at this fab museum!

Flag and symbols

This is the flag of the UK. It was created in 1801.

As you can see, the flag has three colors—red, white, and blue. There's a special flag for each saint, and the UK flag combines the flags of the patron saints of England, Scotland, and Ireland.

The UK flag is usually called the **Union Jack**.

Some other countries (and states/provinces) use the Union Jack on their flags too. This is because in the past they were part of the **British Empire**—and were ruled by Britain.

Did you know?
Wales is not represented in the UK's flag. That's because when the flag was designed, Wales wasn't yet part of the UK.

This is the **Royal Coat of Arms of the UK**.

What two animals can you see in the Coat of Arms?

________________ ________________

Answers: Lion and Unicorn

Animal symbols of the UK are the **lion** and the **bulldog**.

Did you know?
The motto at the bottom of the Coat of Arms is not written in English! It is actually written in French! It means "*God and my right.*"

Does your country have any special symbols?

____

What animal is on the Coat of Arms and is also a symbol of the UK? ________________

Answer: Lion

How to buy things in the UK

The type of money that a country uses is called its currency. The UK's currency is the pound sterling—or just the "pound."

There are 100 pennies (called pence) in a pound. (Pence is often shortened to "p".)

Coins come in amounts of 1p, 2p, 5p, 10p, 20p, and 50p. There are also 1-pound and 2-pound coins. Notes (or bills) come in the values of 5, 10, 20, and 50 pounds.

The queen's picture is on all notes and coins.

You may notice that some coins and notes have different pictures. That's because some are newer styles, but the older coins and notes are still used too.

Some of the coins were made so that you could fit together the 50p, 20p, 10p, 5p, 2p, and 1p coins to create a picture of a shield! The 1-pound coin shows the full shield.

Did you know?
Every coin shows the year it was produced.
Can you find a coin that was made in the year you were born?

Did you know?
A shape with seven sides is called a heptagon.

Quizzes!

A. What is the smallest value of coin? ______________

B. What is the biggest value of coin? ______________

C. What is the biggest value of note? ______________

D. What is the smallest value of note? ______________

E. How many sides does a 50p coin have? ______________

F. Whose picture is on all notes and coins? ______________

G. What color is the 20-pound note? ______________

Answers: A- 1 pence; B- 2 pounds; C- 50 pounds; D- 5 pounds; E- 7; F- The queen; G- Purple

Leonardo drew a pound symbol. Can you copy him?

History of England—lots of battles and wars!

England has a long and very colorful history! The country has been captured and occupied by many different groups over time. And, in turn, England has conquered plenty of other countries too!

Leonardo will tell you about some of the main events in this fascinating history:

Invasions

The Romans invaded England as far back as 55 BC! They ruled England for 400 years, and there are still many Roman ruins all around the country today.

In 1066 AD, France captured England. There was a very famous battle called the Battle of Hastings. France's king then became the King of England!

A deadly disaster!

Between the 1340s and 1350s, a devastating plague killed almost one-third of England's population!

Power hungry

In the 1400s and 1500s, England conquered many other countries, creating a large global empire. England held power in the USA, Australia, New Zealand, Singapore, India ... and other places! England also conquered Wales!

Not-so-friendly neighbors! (who then became friends ...)

Throughout history, there were many battles between England, Scotland, and Wales.

Then in 1707, England and Scotland joined together under one leadership and became Great Britain. Ireland joined them in 1801, but then left again in 1921.

55 BC
1066 AD
1340
1400s & 1500s
1921

Leonardo is a little bit confused ... Can you help him to put the events of England's long history in order?

History of Scotland—
from the Ice Age to today—clans, kings, and battles

People have lived in Scotland since the end of the Ice Age—that was around 10,000 years ago!

Did you know?
There are many castles in Scotland. These were built to keep invaders out!

Roman invasions

By the first century AD, a lot of what is now Scotland was part of the mighty Roman Empire. But the Romans never conquered Scotland's northern territory. It was called Caledonia, and the Romans called its native people "Picti"—or "painted"—because they painted their bodies!

The Romans built a huge wall—which they named Hadrian's Wall, after their Emperor—to keep the Picti people away. You can still walk along Hadrian's Wall today!

Scots are from ... Ireland?!?!

Later, the land was invaded by Scots people—who came from Ireland!

Kingdoms combined

Several rival kingdoms joined together in the ninth century to create the Kingdom of Scotland. They fought many wars with England!

Unity

In the 1700s, Scotland and England joined together with one parliament, although Scotland kept its own religion and legal system.

Take a picture of a magnificent Scottish castle.

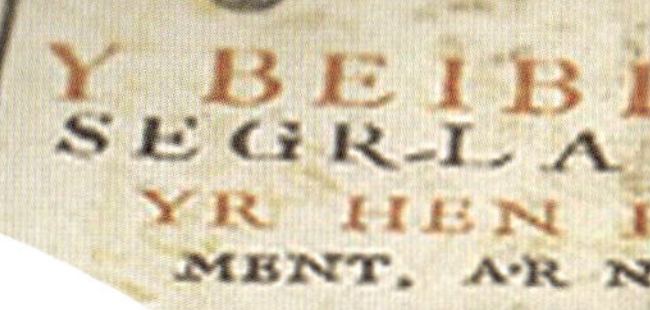

History of Wales—
land of legends, dragons, castles, and fights!

Early humans lived in the land now known as Wales many thousands of years ago. During the Ice Age, large mammoths and reindeer roamed freely.

Let Leonardo take you on an adventure through Wales's exciting history!

Celts, Druids, and magic!

Around 1000 BC, people called Celts came from other parts of Europe to the area that is now Wales. You can still see many Celtic influences in Wales today. The Celts were led by Druids—a type of priests. They followed a religion based on nature and magic!

Invasions and castles

Wales was invaded many times—by the Romans, the Saxons, the English, and the Normans, to name just a few! Many castles were built across the country to protect the lands from outside invaders. Today, the remains of 600 old castles can be found around the country!

Myths and legends

Have you ever heard of King Arthur and the Knights of the Round Table? Or the magical Kingdom of Camelot? Or Merlin the Wizard? These tales all have roots in Welsh history and legend!

Another popular Welsh legend is the **red dragon** and the white dragon ... Merlin the Wizard said that the white dragon of the Saxons would rule Wales at first, but would then be defeated by the red dragon!

Can you draw Merlin the Wizard and a dragon?

History of Northern Ireland—
troubled times and a country divided

Northern Ireland and the Republic of Ireland were once one united country. Leonardo will tell you more about Ireland's past, and how it eventually split into two:

The English connection

In 1170, the English first took an interest in Ireland's affairs. After the English helped the Irish in a battle, they were **given land** in Ireland as a reward.

At first the English controlled just a small part of the country. But in 1541, the King of England made himself **King of Ireland** too. That led to many **fights**!

In 1801, Ireland was officially joined with England, Scotland, and Wales to create the **Union of Great Britain and Ireland**. But many troubles followed ...

Starvation

The Irish potato crop failed for several years in the mid-1800s. This caused a **huge famine** in Ireland, and many people starved to death. It's known as the **Potato Famine**. The English wouldn't help the starving people, and this made the Irish hate the English even more!

Separate countries

In 1948, the Republic of Ireland became an **independent** country. Northern Ireland stayed with the UK. There were troubles, though, until the 1990s.

Quizzes!

1. What reward were the English given in 1170?

A. Bread

B. Gold

C. Land

D. Money

2. A lack of which food caused the big famine?

A. Carrots

B. Fish

C. Burgers

D. Potatoes

Answers: 1. C.; 2. D.

Being royal ... about the Royal Family

The Royal Family means all the close members of the queen's large family. The current queen is called Queen Elizabeth the Second.

Can you guess why she is called the Second?

____

Answer: She is the second queen named Elizabeth.

What's in a name?

The Royal Family has had several last names over the years, including Tudor, Stuart, Hanover, and Wessex. These last names are often called Houses. The current Royal Family's last name is Windsor—or the House of Windsor.

Who will be next?

When a king or queen dies or steps down, their oldest child becomes the next king or queen. If the king or queen has no children, there are complicated rules—called the order of succession—that decide who is next in line for the throne.

Did you know?
King Henry the 8th is known for having lots of wives—he had six!

Did you know?
The queen has different homes all over the UK. Her main home is Buckingham Palace in London. She also has three other official homes, and several other places where she stays sometimes.

Does your country have a king or queen? Yes / No

Did your country have a royal family in the past? Yes / No

Would you like to be a royal?
Yes / No / Maybe ...

Here is a beautiful crown for you to color.

WE'VE TALKED A LOT ABOUT THE UK, NOW LET'S TALK ABOUT THE PEOPLE FROM THE UK!

Culture and customs

The UK really is a big mixture of many different cultures and customs! All four countries have their own very different ways and traditions.

Many other groups have also chosen to move to the UK over the years, and they brought their own customs with them. The cultures of other European countries have influenced the UK too.

Leonardo will tell you some interesting things about British culture:

- The normal greeting is a handshake, although hugs are now very common between friends.
- British people are often said to be quite reserved. This means they don't show lots of emotions in public. This can make them seem pretty formal and dull at times! But they're not really!
- Many Brits don't like to hold eye contact for long.
- Brits are known for drinking lots of tea!

TIP!

Don't assume that everyone you meet is English! People from the other countries in the UK can be quite proud of their roots, and they do not like being called English. It is better to call everyone British.

Look around you ... can you help Leonardo find more customs from the UK?

____

____

____

CORNWALL CHEESE COOPER'S HILL PLYMOUTH

UK superstitions

There are lots of superstitions in the UK!
Leonardo will tell you about some of them. (Do you have any of these in your country?)

Breaking a **mirror** brings seven years' bad luck!

Opening an **umbrella** inside is bad luck. So is walking under a **ladder**, spilling **salt**, and putting **new shoes** on a table!

Lucky things include **black cats**, **horseshoes** (but only the right way up!), four-leafed **clovers**, and touching **wood**!

Try to take a picture of a black cat.

Do you know of any other UK superstitions?

____

____

Does your country have any superstitions?

____

Do you know what a **magpie** is? It's a black-and-white bird. In the UK, seeing magpies means different things, depending on how many of them you see. There is even a rhyme to help people remember! *"One for sorrow, Two for joy, Three for a girl, Four for a boy ..."*

(This means seeing one magpie is unlucky, but two are lucky. Three magpies mean a baby girl will be born, and four mean a baby boy!)

BON APPETIT!

Eating in the UK

Traditional meals in most parts of the UK were made up of meat, potatoes, and two different kinds of vegetables. Times have changed though, and now you can find food from all over the world in the UK.

There are still several dishes that are special to the UK, and some that are common to each of the different countries within the UK. Even more meals are specialties of different regions in the UK.

Let Leonardo introduce you to some of the UK's wonderful food

Roast Dinner

The roast dinner is sometimes called the UK's national dish. It is traditionally eaten on a Sunday, so it's also known as a Sunday roast.

It includes roasted meat, different kinds of vegetables, roast potatoes, and gravy. Depending on what meat is served, other items can vary.

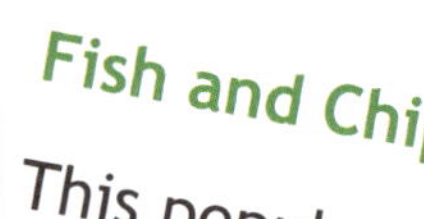

Fish and Chips

This popular meal consists of batter-coated fried fish and chips (deep-fried potatoes similar to french fries). Takeaway shops traditionally sold it wrapped up in newspaper!

Some people eat fish and chips with gravy, mushy peas, or curry sauce.

Did you know?
Putting your elbows on the table when you eat is considered quite impolite in the UK!

Haggis

Haggis is a Scottish dish. Traditionally, it is made by stuffing a sheep's stomach with other parts of a sheep—and a mixture of onion, spices, oatmeal, suet, and gravy.

Do you want to try it?
Yes___ No___ Maybe___

What's your favorite food from the UK?

____

BON APPETIT!

Pies, pasties, and puddings

Pies and pasties

Have you tasted a pie in England? Is it different from the pies in your country? English pies and pasties are similar—both contain a different selection of meats and vegetables, surrounded with a pastry crust. Pasties are supposed to be a meal on their own. Pies usually come with chips or mashed potatoes, vegetables, and gravy.

Soda bread

Common in Northern Ireland, soda bread is delicious and fluffy!

Did you know?

A pasty in Northern Ireland is different than a pasty in England. In Northern Ireland, it is similar to a burger.

Cooked breakfast

You might also hear this called a "fry-up" —because most of the items are fried!

A cooked breakfast can contain a combination of many things. Some of the most popular are bacon, sausages, fried eggs or scrambled eggs, fried mushrooms and tomatoes, hash browns, baked beans, fried bread or toast, and black pudding.

Did you know?

Black pudding is actually made from pig's blood!

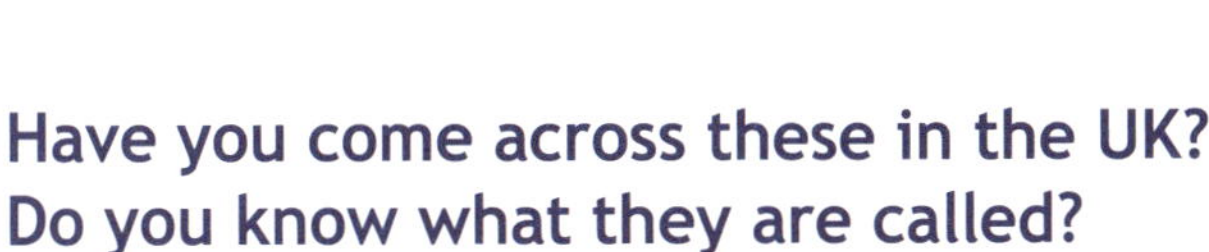

Have you come across these in the UK? Do you know what they are called?

Answer: Crumpets

Draw on the plate what you ate for breakfast this morning.

Even MORE fabulous food!

Scones

Scones are a very English or Welsh treat. They are like small, heavy, thick cakes, usually served with jam and cream. They are often enjoyed in the afternoon with a pot of tea.

Did you know?

The sandwich was invented in the UK, near London. The Earl of Sandwich was too busy to stop playing a card game, so he asked his staff to bring him some meat between two pieces of bread!

Take a picture of your favorite UK meal.

Help Leonardo find these different foods:

- ☐ Bread
- ☐ Cheese
- ☐ Meat
- ☐ Pie
- ☐ Chicken
- ☐ Fish
- ☐ Chips
- ☐ Potato
- ☐ Apple
- ☐ Scone
- ☐ Peas
- ☐ Pasty

I	E	S	A	E	P	N	R	I	T
E	L	G	D	A	E	R	B	Y	P
N	P	A	S	K	H	M	H	W	O
O	P	M	C	H	E	E	S	E	T
C	A	I	J	W	I	A	I	H	A
S	H	N	E	E	N	T	F	S	T
C	A	P	A	S	T	Y	C	U	O

What's your favorite food from your country?

____

____

____

Language in the UK

English is the most widely spoken language in the UK. It is the first language of many other countries around the world too. And it's one of the most-learned second languages all around the globe.

Did you know?

Many other languages are spoken in the UK besides English! Some people in Wales speak Welsh. In Northern Ireland, people may speak Irish and Ulster Scots. And some people in Scotland speak Scottish Gaelic, which is very similar to Ulster Scots.

Different groups of immigrants over the years have also brought their own languages with them. There are entire UK communities that speak Chinese, Polish, Arabic, Urdu ... and many, many more!

DIA DUIT!
(Irish)

Leonardo can say hello in Irish and Welsh! Can you say hello in any other languages? Write in the speech bubbles.

Many influences

The English language has been shaped by many other languages throughout history. It has taken lots of words from other languages too!

Variations

"Accents" are differences in how English is pronounced in different areas. But "dialect" is more than just a different accent. A dialect has words and phrases that are only used in one particular area.

Strange facts about the English language

Sometimes people from different parts of the UK have trouble understanding each other because of their different accents and dialects.

Did you know?

Long ago, French was actually the main language in England for a while!

***Bap*, *Batch*, *Cob*, *Barm*, *Muffin*, *Bridie*, *Rowie*, *Stottie*, and *Oggie* are all words used in different parts of the UK for the same type of food. Can you guess which food it is?**

Answer: B – They are all different words used for bread rolls!

Can you think of any more English idioms?

____

____

____

Interesting idioms

Do you know what an idiom is?

It's a phrase that means something different than the actual words. English is full of fabulous idioms. Leonardo will share some with you:

"It's Raining Cats and Dogs"
Don't worry—there are no cats or dogs about to fall on you! This means it's raining really hard!

"A Piece of Cake"
If you can't see an actual piece of cake, this phrase means that something is very easy to do.

"Hold Your Horses"
Don't panic, nobody REALLY wants you to hold back any horses! This means to wait and be patient.

"Let the Cat Out of the Bag"
There's no cat in a bag really ... This means to let a secret slip out by accident.

Can you draw a cool picture to show another one of these idioms?

Fun facts! What's the biggest, fastest, oldest ...?

Everyone's interested in all the strange and unique things that make a place special, right? So let's have a look at some of these interesting things from the UK!

Windsor Castle is the **biggest and oldest** castle in the world that still has people living in it!

Cumberland Pencil Museum is home to the **longest colored pencil** on the planet! It is eight meters (**26** feet) long!

London is the **only city** to have hosted the Olympic Games **three times**!

Scotland is said to be home to a large and mysterious water creature—called the **Loch Ness Monste**r! Each year, a million people visit Loch Ness to try to spot **Nessie**.

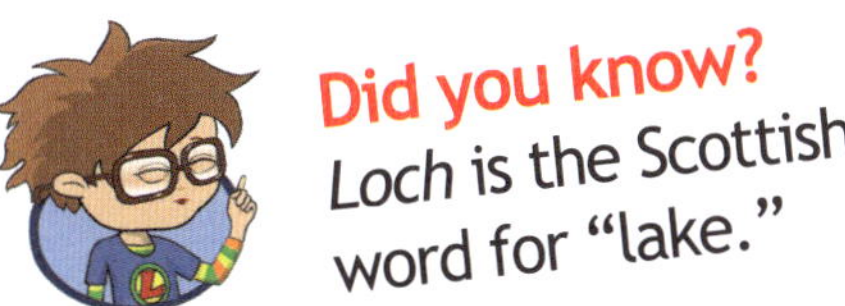

Did you know?
Loch is the Scottish word for "lake."

What do you think the Loch Ness Monster would look like? Can you draw it in the box?

Can you believe it!? Even MORE fun facts!

No place in the UK is more than 120 km (75 miles) from the sea!

A place in Wales has the **longest name** in Europe, and one of the longest place names in the world: **"Llanfairpwllgwyngyllgogerychwyrndrobwllllantysiliogogogoch."** Try to say it!

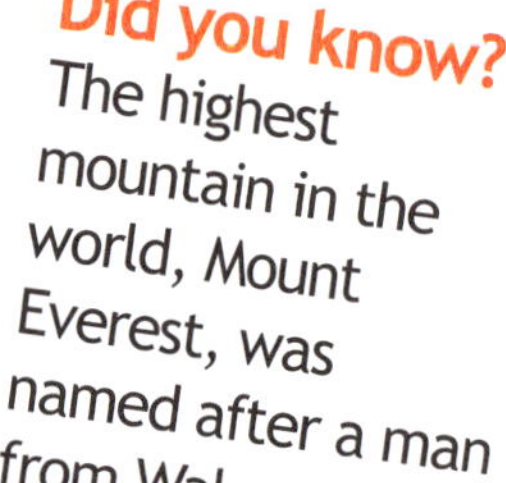

Did you know?
The highest mountain in the world, Mount Everest, was named after a man from Wales. Mount Everest is in Nepal.

In 2015, **Queen Elizabeth II** broke Queen Victoria's record, and became the UK's longest-reigning monarch. Elizabeth II has now been queen for over **63 years!**

The world's biggest **prawn cocktail** was made in the UK.

There is a **butterfly** named after the UK's flag—it's called the **Union Jack**. But … the butterfly comes from Australia!

Bala Lake in Wales is home to a rare type of **fish** called the **gwyniad**. This is thought to be the only place in the world where these fish live.

Can you remember the colors of the Union Jack? Color this butterfly using the flag's colors.

Quizzes!

1. Who was the longest reigning UK monarch?

____

2. What is the Australian butterfly named after?

____

3. What country is Mount Everest in?

____

Answers: 1. Queen Victoria; 2. UK's flag (the Union Jack); 3. Nepal

Lots of sports

Football

The most popular sport in the UK is football, also known as soccer. Many people believe it was actually started in England, although the modern game of football is very different than the early game where people just kicked a ball around!

There are more than 100 teams in the UK's football league, although only the best 20 play in the top league—the Premiership League.

Do you know any famous football teams from the UK?

____

____

Do you have a favorite team? ____________________

Help Leonardo to figure out which sports are team sports and which are individual sports (where you play on your own, usually against one other person).

Tennis, Netball, Rugby, Football, Volleyball, Badminton, Cricket, Table Tennis, Hockey, Basketball, Baseball.

Team

Answers - Team:
Netball, Rugby, Football,
Volleyball, Cricket, Hockey,
Basketball, Baseball

Individual

Answers - Individual:
Tennis, Badminton, Table
Tennis

Cricket

Cricket—a bat-and-ball game—is the national sport of the UK. It spread all around the world after its birth in England.

Rugby

Rugby is a rough sport (American football came from rugby). In the past, rugby was mainly played by the upper classes. But today, anyone can play. It is especially popular in Wales. There are two types of rugby—League and Union—and each has different rules.

Other popular sports in the UK include tennis, badminton, swimming, netball, and rowing.

Leonardo loves tennis! What is your favorite sport to play or do?

____

What is your favorite sport to watch?

____

What sports are popular in your country?

____

____

Brainy UK trivia quiz!

What four countries make up the UK? ______________ ,

______________ , ______________ , ______________

What is the UK's capital city? ______________

What is Edinburgh's nickname? ______________

Where can you find bagpipes? ______________

What city is home to Llandaff Cathedral? ______________

What color is the dragon on the Welsh flag? ______________

What is the capital city of Northern Ireland? ______________

What is the nickname of the UK's flag? ______________

What is the currency of the UK? ______________

Who is shown on all UK money? ______________

How many types of rugby are there? ______________

How do people usually greet each other? ______________

What should you keep off tables at mealtimes? ______________

Answers: 1. England, Scotland, Wales, and Northern Ireland; 2. London; 3. Auld Reekie; 4. Scotland; 5. Cardiff; 6. Red; 7. Belfast; 8. Union Jack; 9. Pound Sterling; 10. The queen; 11. Two; 12. Handshake 13. Elbows

More brainy UK trivia quiz!

Where were Scots people originally from? ________________________

The rare creatures that live in Bala Lake are a type of what? ______________

What black pet is said to be lucky?________________________

What is the Queen's first name? ________________________

What part of the UK suffered from a terrible potato famine? ______________

What is a lock? ______________________

Complete this idiom: "It's raining _______ and _______ ."

Was cricket invented in England, Scotland, Wales or Northern Island? ________
____

Who hides pots of gold at the end of the rainbow? ____________________

Where is soda bread popular? ________________________

What dish is popular? Fish and ________

What country's flag is blue with a white cross? ______________

Answers: 14. Ireland; 15. Fish; 16. Cat; 17. Elizabeth;
19. Ireland; 19. Lake; 20. Cats and Dogs;
21. England; 22. Leprechauns; 23. Northern Ireland;
24. Chips; 25. Scotland

Fun Page!

You already know that one of the UK's national animals is the lion ... so here's a lovely lion for you to color.

Now give it an awesome name! 

My lion is called ____________________

Can you draw a line to match the balls to their sports?

1. Football
2. Rugby
3. Tennis
4. Basketball
5. Golf
6. Cricket

A

B

C

D

E

F

Answers: 1. E, 2. F, 3. A, 4. C, 5. B, 6. D

Funny money!

If you have 10 pounds and you buy a T-shirt for 5 pounds, a toy for 2 pounds, and a pencil for 50p, how much change will you get back?

____

If you want to buy a key ring for 75p, what coins do you need to use the fewest coins AND give the exact money?

____

Leonardo buys a shirt for 15 pounds, a toy for 5 pounds, a chocolate bar for 1 pound, a bottle of water for 1 pound, and a pencil for 30p. What is his total bill?

____

Answers: 2 pounds and 50 pence; 50p + 20p + 5p; 22 pounds and 30 pence

How many words can you make from "Buckingham Palace"? For example: "cup":

____

____

____

LONDON
HERE WE COME!

Before you start reading about London ...

What do you already know about this city?

____

____

____

What are you most hoping to see and do in London?

____

____

____

Are you excited about the trip?

This is an excitement indicator. Ask your family members how excited they are (from "not at all" up to "very, very much"), and mark each of their answers on the indicator. Leonardo has already marked the level of his excitement ...

Leonardo

not at all

very very much!

WELCOME TO LONDON !!!

London is a lively and exciting city with so much to see and do! It's the capital city of both England and the whole United Kingdom (UK). London is located in the southern part of England. You'll see the River Thames running through the city. The Thames is the second longest river in the UK.

London has had a few nicknames over the years—the most popular is **"The Smoke,"** or sometimes **"The Big Smoke."** That's because Londoners used to heat their homes by burning coal—and the city also had lots of factories—so the air was very smoky! Sometimes it was hard to breathe.

In the 1960s, London was often called **"The Swinging City."** It was the center of "mod" fashion and popular music.

London is a very **multicultural and multinational** city. This means that people from lots of different nations, with lots of different cultures, live in the city. Some of the different groups have been living in London for many years—and new people are still coming to the city from all over the world.

London is now home to around **8.6 million** people!

What is the capital city of your country?

____

Does it have a nickname?

____

Do any major rivers flow through your country's capital city?

____

What is the main language in your country?

____

London city map

Greater London is HUGE! It is divided into several different areas that are called **boroughs**. A borough is like a small town or district—it's a smaller piece of the whole area. There are 32 London boroughs, plus the City of London.

The main tourist spots can be found in the central part of the city, although there are plenty of great things to do in the outer areas too!

Did you know?
A major highway—the M25—runs all around the edge of Greater London. The M25 is often called the London Orbital, because of the way it seems to orbit around the city!

What places are you really looking forward to seeing in London?

____

____

____

Can you circle them on the map?

Can you also put a star where your hotel is?

The historic heart of London is the old City of London. The old city is actually the smallest city in the UK! It is often called the "Square Mile."
Can you guess why?!

Answer: The old City of London is just around one square mile in size!

London's very long history

Who built London?

The old City of London was built by **Romans** who invaded Britain. It was a really small city back then ... The Romans called it **"Londinium."**

A city destroyed

An army led by a British queen named Boudica forced the Romans out of London. Then Boudica had the city **burned down**! But the Romans came back and rebuilt London, adding a wall around it for protection. They left in the fifth century.

French invasions and hard lives

People from **France**, called the Normans, captured London in the Middle Ages. They built the Tower of London. Life in London was very hard. It was a **dirty** and **smelly** place, with lots of sickness.

Leonardo wants to tell you more!

1600s: This was a VERY bad time for London. Guy Fawkes tried to **blow up** the Houses of Parliament! There was a **civil war** and the king was **beheaded**! The **Great Plague** killed thousands of people, and **the Great Fire of London** destroyed nearly 80 percent of the city.

1700s: London grew more powerful and became an important **financial center.**

1800s: Under **Queen Victoria**, London got a lot bigger and became an important **industrial city**. But life for poor people was very bad.

Did you know?

The part of London where you'll find Buckingham Palace, the Houses of Parliament, London Zoo, and many other famous spots used to be a separate city called the **City of Westminster**!

Did you know?

People celebrate with fireworks and bonfires every year on the 5th of November—the day Guy Fawkes was arrested. **Guy Fawkes Day** was started to show thanks that he was captured!

Things to see only in London

There are LOTS of fantastic things to see in London!

The city combines old historic places with great modern spots. The streets are very busy, but you can also find large grassy parks where you can run and play. There are hundreds of museums and art galleries, theme parks, zoos, old churches ... and more!

London has many different shops and markets, and it is the home of one very special shop—Hamleys Toy Store. This magical place is the oldest toy store in the whole world!

You can see the queen's main home in London—Buckingham Palace. The dazzling Crown Jewels are also kept in London.

Did you know?
London is known for its special types of guards that protect important places. The guards at Buckingham Palace wear red and black uniforms with big black furry hats. The guards at the Tower of London are called Beefeaters, and they also wear a special uniform. You won't find these guards anywhere else in the UK!

Quizzes!

1. What is the oldest toy shop in the world called?

____

2.What people guard the Tower of London?

____

3. What is the queen's main home called?

____

Answers: 1. Hamleys, 2. Beefeaters, 3. Buckingham Palace

Getting to and from London—by air and undersea!

Leonardo wants to tell you about some of the ways to get to and from London ... there are lots!

Planes

London has a whopping FIVE airports! The main airport is Heathrow. This is the biggest and busiest airport in the UK—and in all of Europe. It's also one of the busiest airports in the world! The other London airports are called Gatwick, Luton, Stanstead, and London City.

Trains

Do you like trains? London is well connected to the rest of the UK by train. Some of the major train stations are called Euston, Victoria, Waterloo, King's Cross, St. Pancras, Liverpool Street, Charing Cross, and Paddington.

You can also get from London to many cities in Europe by train—on a railway that goes under the sea! The train is called the Eurostar, and it goes through the Channel Tunnel (a tunnel built under the English Channel). It's the longest undersea tunnel in the world!

Did you know?
When you combine all of its airports, London is the busiest city in the world for flights!

Did you know?
The Channel Tunnel's name is often shortened to just "the Chunnel"!

Have you ever heard of Paddington Bear?

Paddington Bear is a story character. He was sent to England from "deepest, darkest Peru," and he arrived at Paddington Station. That is how he got his name! He has many adventures, and he's very popular with children in the UK.

Paddington Bear located in Paddington Station

Getting around in London!

Buses

There are many buses that travel to different parts of London and beyond. Traditional London buses are very famous—they are bright red and have two levels. That's why they're called double-deckers.

Snap a picture of a red double-decker.

London Underground

The London Underground is a type of **fast subway system**. As the name shows, it runs underground! It connects almost all parts of the city, and it's one of the best ways to get between places. There are no traffic jams on the London Underground!

There are many different lines (or routes) on the London Underground, and the maps look quite confusing! Once you get the hang of it though, it's actually very easy!

Taxis

There are regular taxis in London, just as you will find in almost every major city around the world. But London also has a special type of taxi—the big **black hackney cab**. These replaced horse-drawn carriages as a way to get around the city streets.

Did you know?

The nickname of the London Underground is **"the Tube"**!

What transportation have you used in London?

____

____

What is your favorite type of London transport?

____

Which of these is NOT a famous type of transport in London?

Answer: B is not a famous type of transportation in London.

Buckingham Palace:
Home of the queen!

Buckingham Palace was built in 1703, and it has been the official Royal home since the 1830s.

It is a grand and elegant building that is surrounded by a metal fence. Even by just peeking through the fence you can see how marvelous it is!

How many words can you make from "Buckingham Palace"?
For example: "ice"

___

___

___

Changing of the Guard

The palace is protected by Royal Guards. Every few days, there is an elaborate ceremony where new guards march to the palace with a band! They swap places with the old guards, who can then go back to their base.

TIP!

Ask your parents to check the schedule for the Changing of the Guard, because it changes throughout the year.

Did you know?

There are 775 rooms inside Buckingham Palace! And there are 52 bedrooms for the Royal Family and their guests!

Did you know?

The queen likes a type of dog called a corgi. She has owned around 30 corgis in her life!

Quizzes!

1. Can you guess how many bathrooms are in the palace?

A. 18 B. 38 C. 78 D. 108

2. How many bedrooms do you think there are for the palace's staff?

A. 92 B. 114 C. 159 D. 188

Answers: 1. C, 2. D

The Tower of London—
a 900-year-old castle

The majestic Tower of London was built in **1066** by French Normans who captured London. It's surrounded by a **moat** and **high walls** for protection. Back then, the local people hated it!

Over the years, the tower has been used in many ways. It's been a **home for the Royals**—and a famous prison where two of King Henry VIII's wives were beheaded! It's also been a **mint** (place where money is made), a place to **store weapons**, and even a **zoo!**

Today, the tower is guarded by **Beefeaters,** and it is home to some big birds called **ravens.** It has lots of interesting displays. Leonardo recommends that you see the sparkling **Crown Jewels**—over 23,000 jewels worth about £20 billion (or $30 billion)!

Did you know?
A superstition says there must always be at least six ravens at the Tower of London ... or it will fall down! How many ravens did you see?

Can you help Leonardo find all these words that are connected with the Tower of London?

- ☐ Castle
- ☐ Prison
- ☐ Zoo
- ☐ Jewels
- ☐ Raven
- ☐ Moat
- ☐ Walls
- ☐ Mint
- ☐ Home
- ☐ Beefeater

A	C	R	S	H	K	L	G	V	M
E	M	O	H	S	X	S	Z	I	C
N	N	M	A	L	T	O	N	I	N
O	E	O	A	L	O	T	O	N	B
S	V	A	C	A	S	T	L	E	A
I	A	T	A	W	R	K	A	P	I
R	R	E	T	A	E	F	E	E	B
P	N	A	L	J	E	W	E	L	S

Take a picture of a raven!

London's grand and gorgeous religious places

London is filled with beautiful old churches and other religious buildings. Because of its many different cultures, London also has mosques, Hindu temples, Buddhist temples, synagogues, gurdwaras,* and more!

**Gurdwaras are Sikh (seek) temples. Sikhism began in India. It's the fifth most popular religion in the world.*

Two of the most famous religious buildings are Westminster Abbey and St. Paul's Cathedral. Both are very popular places for tourists to visit.

Westminster Abbey

This was built in the 1240s, but there had been a church at that same place for many years before.

The building has lots of beautiful details inside and outside. When you go inside, you can also visit the museum and see lots of religious art.

Westminster Abbey is the traditional place where new kings and queens are crowned. It's also where members of the Royal Family are buried when they die. Lots of Royal weddings have been held here. It's where Queen Elizabeth married her husband, Prince Philip (although she wasn't yet queen then). And it's where her grandson, Prince William, married Kate Middleton in 2011.

Did you know?

Eighty-eight churches burned down in the Great Fire of London. Many more were damaged or destroyed during the Reformation (a time when there was lots of fighting within the Christian church). And lots of London churches were also destroyed by bombs during World War II.

St. Paul's Cathedral

This enormous cathedral was built in the 1700s, after the previous church burned down. It stands at the highest point in London, and there has been a church here for more than 1,400 years.

St. Paul's has a beautiful dome on top. Inside, you'll find lots of pretty artwork, statues, and carvings. Many funerals of famous people have taken place here, as well as some Royal weddings.

More stunning sights!

There are many interesting and beautiful landmarks around London. Some are very old and some are quite modern—but all are great places to see when you're in London!

Leonardo wants to tell you about some of his favorites:

The Houses of Parliament

British lawmakers meet in the Houses of Parliament. This is a really long building that sits next to the River Thames. Leonardo likes all the spiky spires and the really tall clock tower.

Tower Bridge

Built in the late 1800s, the beautiful Tower Bridge crosses the River Thames. There are two parts to the bridge—the bottom part can lift up to let tall boats go through. You can walk across the top part and enjoy amazing views!

The Gherkin

This is one of London's most unusual modern buildings—and one of the city's tallest buildings. It opened in 2004. Can you see why it got the nickname "the Gherkin"? It looks like a giant pickle!

Did you know?

Many people think Big Ben is the name of the large clock tower next to the Houses of Parliament. But Big Ben is actually the name of the main bell in the tower. Listen to hear it chime every hour!

What is your favorite London landmark?

____

Why do you like it? What makes it special?

____

____

What are some of the main landmarks in your town or city?

____

____

So much to see at Trafalgar Square

Trafalgar Square is a big public square in the heart of London. It's a great place to get lots of beautiful pictures!

The square is surrounded by amazing buildings, such as the Admiralty Arch, the National Gallery, and St. Martin-in-the-Fields Church. There are interesting statues, fountains, and monuments in the square.

Did you know?
It's against the law to feed the pigeons in Trafalgar Square.

1. Walk to the middle of the square. There is a big statue. Do you know his name?

____

2. What does the man have on his head?

____

3. How many bronze lions are around the bottom?

____

4. What is the man holding in his left hand?

____

Answers: 1. Admiral/Lord Nelson, 2. Hat, 3. Four, 4. Sword

Other statues show important people in the British Navy's past and two old kings. One of the kings is sitting on a horse.

Can you help Leonardo to unscramble these words connected with Trafalgar Square?

Nlsnoe _______________

Lonis _______________

Ssuatet _______________

Pengsio _______________

Fntiosnua _______________

Answers:
Nelson
Lions
Statues
Pigeons
Fountains

Did you know?
The person who designed the fountains at the bottom of the big statue also designed a lot of the buildings in India's capital city, New Delhi.

London's excellent ZOO!

London Zoo is home to LOADS of different cute and interesting animals. Take a stroll through the African zone and see animals like zebras, giraffes, and wild dogs. Wander through the rainforest area and spot lots of creatures in the daylight ... and then in the dark!

You can see the world's largest type of lizard, the fearsome-looking Komodo dragon. Come face-to-face with lions, tigers, penguins, hippos, monkeys, and gorillas—and have fun in the aquarium, the bug house, and the butterfly palace.

There is even a children's zone where you can get up close and friendly with animals like sheep, goats, pigs, and donkeys.

Leonardo recommends trying to make it to the animals' different feeding times.

Did you know? London Zoo is the oldest scientific zoo in the world! The zoo was only for scientific study at first—but it opened to the public in 1847.

Leonardo loves penguins.
What is your favorite zoo animal?

Can you draw your favorite zoo animal?

TIP! Tell your parents how they can save money AND avoid the long lines (or queues). Just buy London Zoo tickets online before your family visits!

More fun with animals!

If you love animals there are plenty of other places in London to make you smile ...

Mudchute Park and Farm

Here you can pet different animals in the petting zoo, feed the ducks, see lots of farm animals in the fields, and ride horses.

Battersea Park Children's Zoo

Leonardo thinks you will LOVE this zoo! It was designed **especially for kids**, and it specializes in smaller animals. There are lemurs, rabbits, pigs, birds, goats, ponies ... and more! There is also a fun play area with lots of **activities and rides**.

Sea Life London Aquarium

This is one of the biggest collections of **fascinating sea creatures** in all of Europe! You can see plenty of creatures from the ocean deep. And there are touch pools where you can find out what some of them actually feel like! (Soft? Sharp? Squishy?)

Can you help Leonardo find these creatures in the word search?

One animal is missing—which one? ____________________

- ☐ Elephant
- ☐ Giraffe
- ☐ Horse
- ☐ Sheep
- ☐ Lion
- ☐ Cow
- ☐ Dog
- ☐ Goat
- ☐ Otter
- ☐ Rabbit
- ☐ Bear
- ☐ Cat
- ☐ Zebra
- ☐ Monkey
- ☐ Deer
- ☐ Bird
- ☐ Tiger
- ☐ Lizard
- ☐ Fish
- ☐ Snake

A	R	B	E	Z	I	G	T	N	C	P	F	A
N	A	I	R	T	E	I	J	A	M	E	I	G
Y	E	R	A	K	N	R	W	O	C	E	S	O
E	B	D	A	N	A	A	O	N	U	H	H	D
K	I	N	A	B	Y	F	H	O	R	S	E	F
N	S	E	B	L	H	F	A	P	I	D	S	L
O	T	I	G	E	R	E	G	I	E	S	O	I
M	T	L	I	Z	A	R	D	E	H	L	I	O
C	H	T	A	O	G	N	R	T	D	E	E	N

Answer: The Otter!

Thrilling theme parks

If you like fun, rides, and laughter galore, you'll LOVE London's different theme parks! These are Leonardo's favorites:

The Making of Harry Potter

Whether you loved the Harry Potter books and movies, or you just love all things magical, the Making of Harry Potter tour is **sure to be spell-binding fun!**

You can stand on the famous train platform and have your **picture taken** with the Hogwarts Express, **see robotic creatures from the movies**, gaze at the **spectacular sets**, spot numerous props, and **learn more** about how the popular Harry Potter films were made.

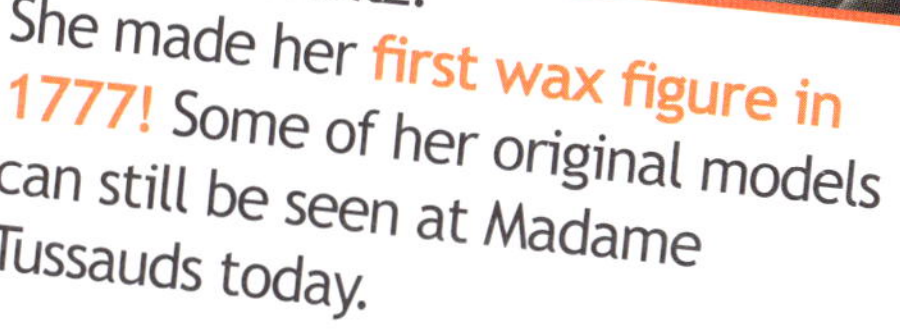

Did you know?
Madame Tussaud was born in France. Her name before she got married was Marie Grosholtz. She made her **first wax figure in 1777!** Some of her original models can still be seen at Madame Tussauds today.

Chessington World of Adventures

This super theme park has more than 40 different rides that will be fun for all your family! There is also a zoo that's packed with many different types of animals and a brilliant aquarium. Plus you'll find plenty of places for your family to stop for a bite to eat or a drink.

Madame Tussauds

Do you want to stand next to all your **favorite movie stars, pop singers,** and **famous athletes?** Perhaps there's a superhero or two that you're crazy about. Maybe you'd like to get close to world leaders, royalty, and well-known faces from the past.

Madame Tussauds has loads of different **lifelike wax models** to amaze you. And that's not all! There is a **fun ride and a thrilling 4D movie theatre**—and a chance to learn more about making the wax figures.

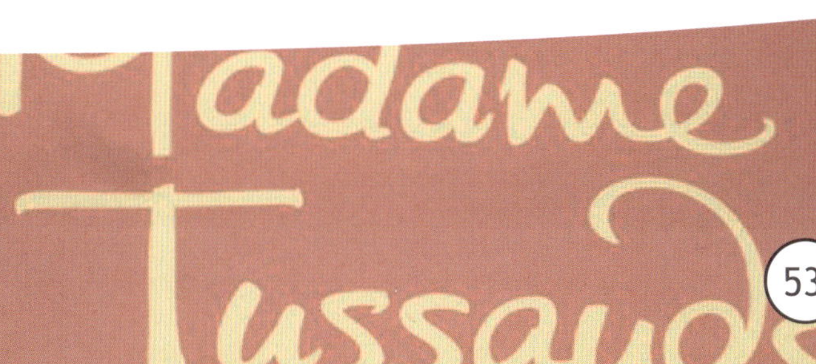

MORE fab theme parks!

Legoland Windsor

Do you like Legos? 🙂 Imagine a place full of things built entirely from Legos! At Legoland Windsor you can feast your eyes on Lego sculptures big and small ... They're sure to give you lots of ideas for your own Lego projects! Miniland is especially fab! Join one of the building workshops and see what you can build yourself with Lego blocks.

There are fun rides too. Many of them let you hop in the driver's seat and drive yourself around! Leonardo thinks you'll really enjoy the great shows and the indoor water-play area. There are lots of places to eat and drink around the park too. It's a really excellent day out!

Wet 'n' Wild at Waterfront Leisure Centre

This is a perfect place if you and your family want to swim and have tons of fun in the water.

Along with a regular swimming pool (for serious swimmers!) and leisure pools (where you can splash and play!!), there is a cool wave machine, an erupting volcano, a waterfall, water jets, and inflatable toys. Race your family to the bottom of the five-lane water slide! If you love speed, the Anaconda flume will be right up your alley!

Can you unscramble these things that you will find at Legoland or Wet 'n' Wild?

Rdise	R _ _ e _
Sileds	_ l _ _ e _
Ssohw	_ h _ _ _
Lgoe	L _ _ _
Splursectu	_ _ u _ _ _ u _ _ s

Answers: Rides, Slides, Shows, Lego, Sculptures

What was your favorite London theme park?

____

What ride did you like the best?

____

What other theme parks have you visited in other places?

____

____

A spooky look at London's past

There are a few places in London that offer lots of **spooky fun.** Be warned though—they can be quite scary!

If you like **heart-pounding adventures**, Leonardo recommends these places for you and your family:

The London Dungeon

Go underground into the murky and **scary depths** of olden-day London. **Be terrified** by some of the city's famous criminals (played by very convincing actors)! The amazing sets and scenery, brilliant special effects, and different sights, sounds, and smells will give you a spine-tingling experience!

There are a few thrilling rides too, and many gory and funny tales to captivate and horrify you!

The London Bridge Experience

Go under the famous bridge and giggle and squeal your way through **London's murky past**. You can see how Queen Boudica battled with the Romans or experience the devastation of the Great Fire of London. **Come face-to-face with notorious criminals**, wander along medieval streets ... and more!

And all that's before you even enter the Tombs! Here, actors wait to give you chilling surprises, and the horrifying sets are designed to give you the creeps!

TIP!

The London Dungeon is designed to be scary fun. If you get really afraid, remember that **they are only actors!** Your parents can also ask one of the actors to lead you outside for a bit. So don't worry!

Looking out from the London Eye

The London Eye is a large **observation wheel** that lets you see far and wide across London. It is a great way to see lots of the famous city sights from above.

Take to the skies in one of the **glass capsules**, and soak up the many wonderful views. The wheel moves slowly, giving you lots of time to spot things and take plenty of pictures!

Did you know?

Leonardo wants to share some interesting facts about the London Eye with you:

- It is a towering 135 meters (443 feet) tall!
- In clear weather you can see for about 40 kilometers (25 miles) in every direction.
- It moves twice as fast as a tortoise sprinting! (That's pretty slow!)
- It took seven years to build!

Take a picture of the stunning London views.

Check off these famous places as you spot them from the London Eye:

- ☐ The Houses of Parliament
- ☐ The River Thames
- ☐ Buckingham Palace
- ☐ The Tower of London
- ☐ Tower Bridge
- ☐ The Gherkin
- ☐ London Zoo
- ☐ St Paul's Cathedral
- ☐ The Oval Cricket Ground
- ☐ Trafalgar Square
- ☐ Hyde Park
- ☐ Westminster Abbey

Time for a break ...
parks, gardens, and play areas

There are lots of places around London where you can run and play, take some time out, and escape from the hurry of city life.

Leonardo likes to unwind in the many different parks, gardens, and play areas all around the city. He wants to tell you about some of his favorites:

Hyde Park

It's one of the biggest parks in London, and has the oldest boating lake in the city.

You can take a boat trip, relax by the water, or feed the ducks and swans that glide around the lake. If the weather is warm, head to the Joy of Life Fountain, where you can splash around in the water yourself!

You'll have lots of fun at the jungle play area too!

Did you know?
Hyde Park is about the same size as the old City of London!

St James's Park

There are lots of birds on the large lake, including big and greedy pelicans! You can watch the pelicans being fed every day at 2:30 p.m.

Cross the bridge to get nice views of the park and the palace.

Here's a duck for you to color. "Quack, quack!"

More places to run around and have heaps of fun!

Regent's Park

There are so many ways to have a great time here! Choose from several playgrounds, a boating lake, a sandpit, tree houses, tennis courts, cafes, vans and stands selling ice cream, and nature galore! What more could you want in a park?!

In the summer months, there are usually many outdoor festivals and live music too.

Richmond Park

If you like Bambi, you'll love seeing all the deer roaming freely in this huge park. It is the biggest of all the Royal Parks, and it has many beautiful plants and flowers to admire. There's a grand old mansion in the park too.

Did you know?

There are eight Royal Parks in London. In the olden days only members of the Royal Family and their guests were allowed to visit them. Now the beautiful green spaces and nature are open to everyone!

Check off these things as you see them in the parks:

- ☐ Duck
- ☐ Swan
- ☐ Flying bird
- ☐ Boat
- ☐ Butterfly
- ☐ Beetle
- ☐ Flower
- ☐ Ice cream
- ☐ Football
- ☐ Umbrella
- ☐ Squirrel
- ☐ Frisbee

What's your favorite color of flower?

____

Make this pretty flower your favorite color.

Even more outdoor fun!

Holland Park

A great place for adventure! Holland Park has loads of stuff for climbing, a tire swing, an exciting zip line, and a giant seesaw! You can see lots of big fish in the pond, as well as pretty Japanese gardens, a waterfall, and an old mansion.

TIP!

Ask your parents to pack a picnic when you go to a park, so you can sit on the grass and enjoy an outdoor lunch!

Do you go to the park a lot at home?

____

What are your favorite things to play on in the park?

____

Which London parks did you visit?

____

____

What was your favorite London park?

____

Complete these things Leonardo likes to play on and play with when he goes to different parks:

S _ _ n _

S _ e _ _ w

S l _ d _

F _ i _ _ e _

F _ _ t _ a _ l

F _ _ e n _ s

C _ r _ u _ _ l

Answers: Swing, Seesaw, Slide, Frisbee, Football, Friends, Carousel

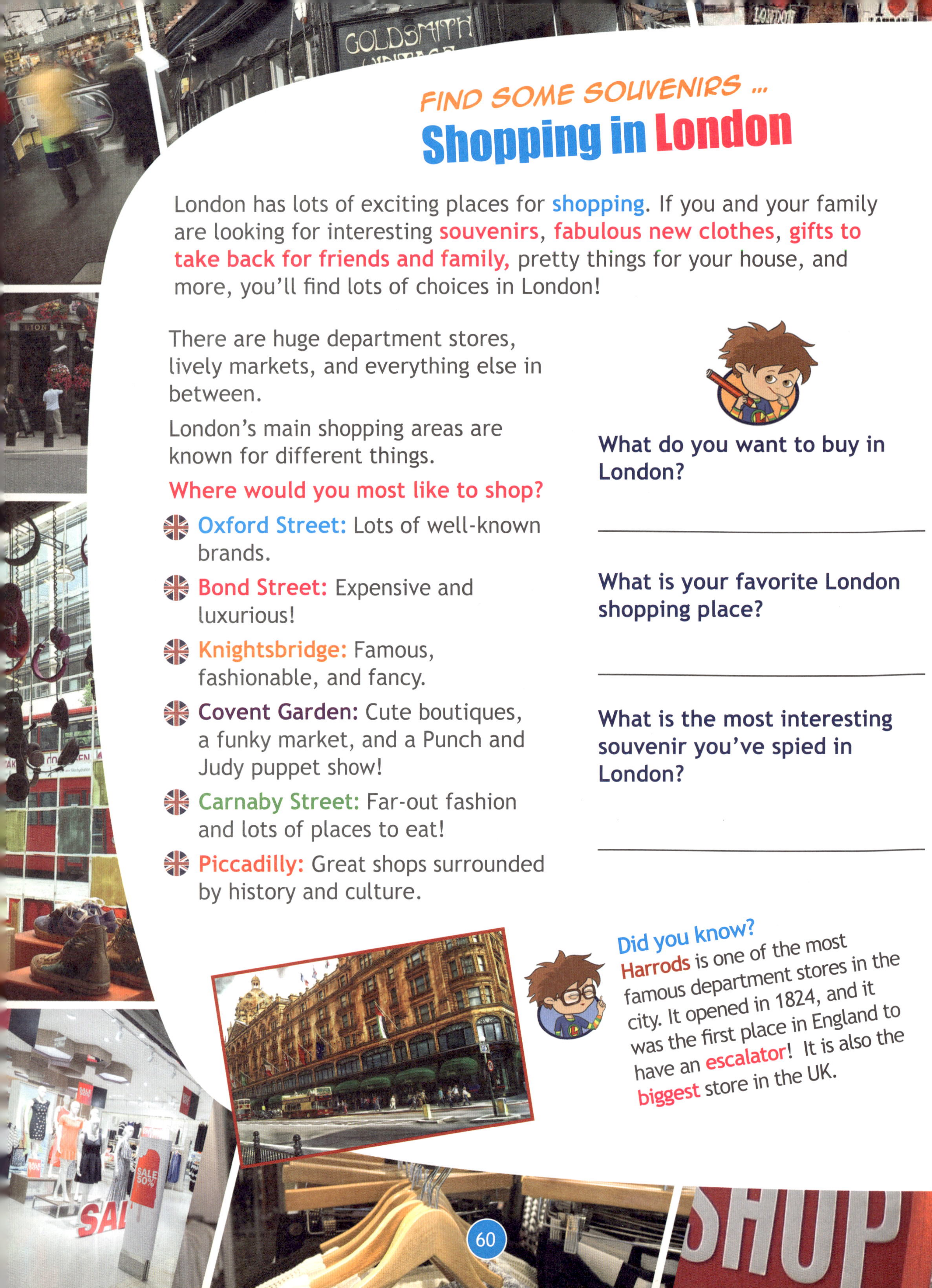

FIND SOME SOUVENIRS ...

Shopping in London

London has lots of exciting places for shopping. If you and your family are looking for interesting souvenirs, fabulous new clothes, gifts to take back for friends and family, pretty things for your house, and more, you'll find lots of choices in London!

There are huge department stores, lively markets, and everything else in between.

London's main shopping areas are known for different things.

Where would you most like to shop?

- **Oxford Street:** Lots of well-known brands.
- **Bond Street:** Expensive and luxurious!
- **Knightsbridge:** Famous, fashionable, and fancy.
- **Covent Garden:** Cute boutiques, a funky market, and a Punch and Judy puppet show!
- **Carnaby Street:** Far-out fashion and lots of places to eat!
- **Piccadilly:** Great shops surrounded by history and culture.

What do you want to buy in London?

____

What is your favorite London shopping place?

____

What is the most interesting souvenir you've spied in London?

____

Did you know?
Harrods is one of the most famous department stores in the city. It opened in 1824, and it was the first place in England to have an escalator! It is also the biggest store in the UK.

PART 2

Shopping in London

Did you know?
Carnaby Street has been a **trendy and popular** part of London for many years. It is known for its **unusual** and independent shops, where you can find some really unique and interesting things.

It was one of the **coolest** parts of London in the 1960s and 1970s. Lots of famous bands and music stars used to hang out here.
Today, it still has a completely different vibe than other parts of London.

Did you know?
Selfridges is the **biggest** department store on **Oxford Street**, and it's the **second biggest store in the UK**. It was **the first place in the world where TV was shown to the public!**

How many words can you make from Carnaby Street? For example: "Can"

____

____

____

If you look above the main entrance, there is a statue of the *Queen of Time*.

1. What color is her dress? ______________
2. What does she have behind her head? ______________
3. How many mermen* are kneeling by her feet? ________
4. What is she holding in her hand? ______________

**Merman: Half-man, half fish*

Answers: 1. Blue and gray; 2. Clock; 3. Two; 4. A ball (with an angel-like figure on it)

Did you know?
Do you like toys? **Hamleys**, the **oldest toy shop in the world**, first opened in 1760! Back then, it was called Noah's Ark. There are more than **50,000** toys and games inside, and you can play with lots of them in the shop!

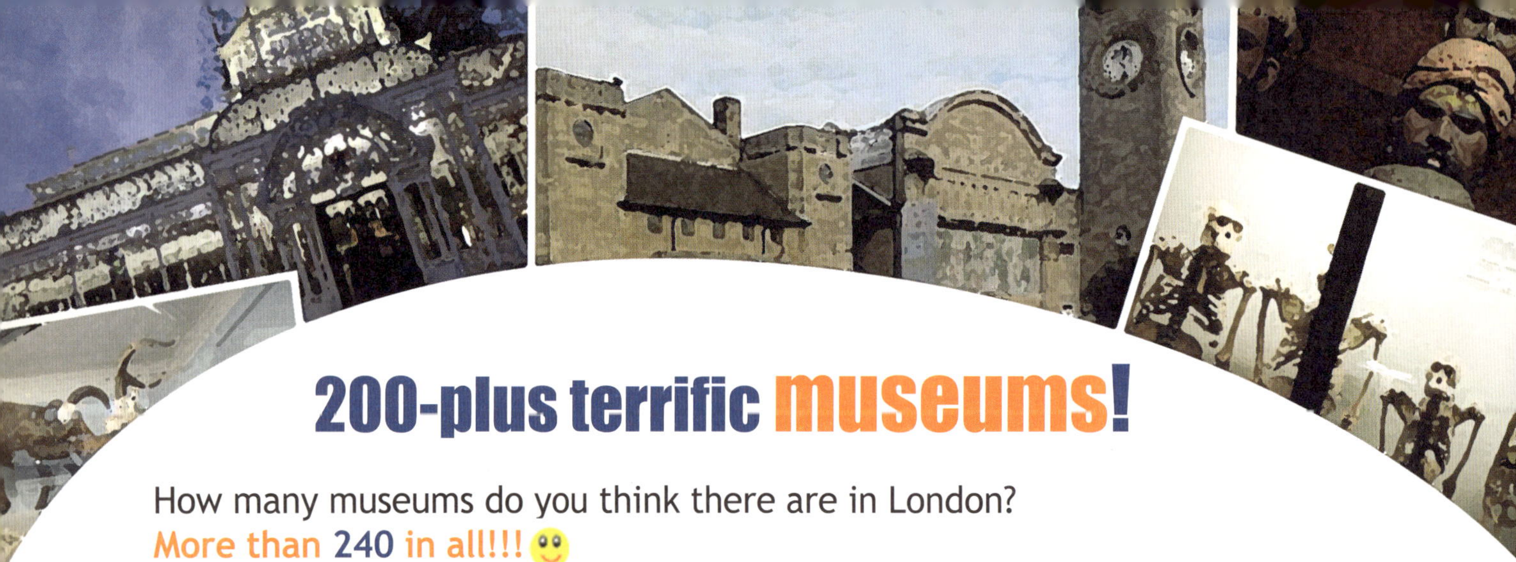

200-plus terrific museums!

How many museums do you think there are in London?
More than 240 in all!!!

There are museums for almost every interest, but Leonardo thinks these are some of the best ones for you and your family:

Horniman Museum

How would you like to come face-to-face with **a giant walrus** ... or see busy bees at work ... or watch beautiful fish? Maybe you'd like to try playing some interesting musical instruments, see lots of artwork, or walk along amazing nature trails?

These are just a few of the cool things waiting for you at the excellent Horniman Museum! **This is one of the best museums in London for kids!**

There are many different, fascinating displays and lots of hands-on activities for you to try!

You can learn more about nature and people, and the large gardens are great for running and playing.

Mark on the scale how cool this museum was:

AMAZING!

Okay

Meh!

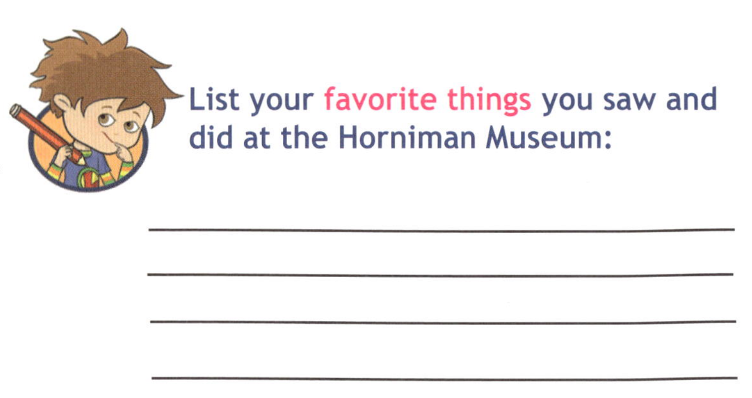

List your favorite things you saw and did at the Horniman Museum:

____

____

____

____

Pirates, mummies, and more !

The Golden Hinde

Do you love pirate stories and the big blue sea? Then step aboard the *Golden Hinde*, matey, and tread the boards of one of the first ships to ever sail all around the world!

There's so much to see and do on this huge reconstructed warship. Leonardo thinks you'll be shouting, "Ahoy there!" in no time at all!

British Museum

Would you like to learn more about ancient Egypt and see a real mummy? What about going back into the mighty Roman Empire or ancient Greece? You can take a journey all around the world—and go through all different time periods—at the fantastic British Museum.

There are hundreds of exciting items and many different displays in the museum's whopping 90-plus rooms!

Did you know?
"Hinde" is the name for a female deer!

Circle the things that are connected with pirates:

CINEMAS
PARROTS
DESERT ISLAND
SHIPS
ANCHOR
SUNGLASSES
ICE CREAM
CARS
HORSE
TREASURE

TIP!

Pick up an activity backpack at the British Museum. It will give you lots of fun things to do as you visit the different displays.

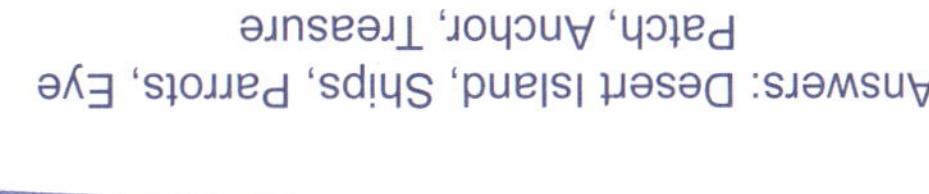

Answers: Desert Island, Ships, Parrots, Eye Patch, Anchor, Treasure

A museum for toys and games!

V & A Museum of Childhood

If you love toys and games, then this hands-on museum is for you!

You can look at lots of **interesting old toys** and see **how kids played in the past**—and check out newer toys too. And there are plenty for you to play with yourself! You can also sit and listen to an **exciting story**, go on **a treasure hunt**, challenge your family to different board games, **ride a rocking horse** ... and more!

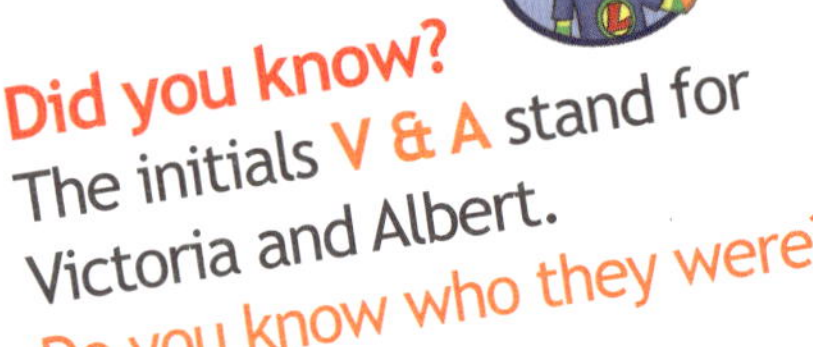

Did you know?
The initials **V & A** stand for Victoria and Albert.
Do you know who they were?

____

____

Answer: Queen Victoria and her husband, Prince Albert.

What museums did you visit in London?

____

____

What was your favorite London museum?

____

What things did you like seeing in the museums?

____

____

____

London theaters and shows you're sure to enjoy ...

The West End is the heart of the London theater scene, where you'll find lots of terrific shows, musicals, and performances. There are many more theaters around the city too, so get ready to be entertained!

Your family will be able to enjoy some excellent shows that are great for all ages!

Leonardo thinks these are especially fab:

Puppet Theatre Barge

Do you like puppets? How about boats? Why not combine the two? Watch a spectacular puppet show as you bob on the River Thames! You and your family can see lots of exciting stories acted out by the beautiful puppets on strings.

Unicorn Theatre

Close to London Bridge, the Unicorn has two great theaters with lots of performances especially for kids. There are also great workshops where you can practice your own acting skills.

Polka Theatre

There's lots to do at this fantastic children's theater. You can watch an entertaining show, join a workshop, have fun in the play area, see interesting displays, and meet other kids!

Have you ever seen a musical before?

____

Have you seen a play before?

____

What shows would you like to see in London?

____

____

London trivia

What is the name of the big observation wheel in London? ________________

Where are the Crown Jewels kept? ________________

Where can you see the Changing of the Guard Ceremony?

____

What should you not feed in Trafalgar Square? ________________

Does Hamleys sell animals, clothes, toys, or books? ________________

What is the name of London's big domed cathedral? ________________

What is Big Ben? ________________

What is the nickname of the London Underground? ________________

What's the nickname of the tall, vegetable-like modern building?

____

What color are traditional London taxis? ________________

Where can you have fun with Lego? ________________

In which park can you see lots of deer? ________________

What museum has a giant walrus? ________________

What is the name of London's River? ________________

What's the biggest store in the UK? ________________

What will fall down if the ravens leave? ________________

Answers: 1. London Eye, 2. Tower of London, 3. Buckingham Palace, 4. Pigeons, 5. Toys, 6. St. Paul's, 7. Bell, 8. The Tube, 9. Gherkin, 10. Black, 11. Legoland, 12. Richmond Park, 13. Horniman, 14. Thames, 15. Harrods; 16. Tower of London

London fun and facts

Have you heard the popular children's song *"London Bridge Is Falling Down"*? Can you sing it? London Bridge has been rebuilt many times over the years. It's a sturdy bridge now, but long ago, parts of an earlier bridge really did fall down!

Have you noticed what color traditional phone booths and mailboxes are in London? (Clue: They are the same color as the traditional buses!)

____

Did you also see what symbol is on both?

____

Color the phone box!

Did you know?
The nickname for a person from London is a "Cockney."

Did you know?
Policemen in London (and the UK) are nicknamed "bobbies"!

Can you find eight differences between these crowns?

Here's a bobby hat ... Can you draw your own face under the hat?

Can you break the code?

Can you crack the code?! Use the key to figure out Leonardo's action-packed journal entry about his trip to London:

A = X, E = Q, O = J, N = 2, D = 5, R = 7, S = 9, P = *, T = #, L = %

People say if you're tired of %J25J2 (_ _ _ _ _ _) then you're tired of life. I really don't know how anyone could be tired of %J25J2 (_ _ _ _ _ _)! There are so many great things to 9QQ (_ _ _) and do. I loved it!!

I spent hours looking at all the incredible toys in HXM%QY9 (_ _ _ _ _ _ _) and a whole day watching different animals at %J25J2 ZJJ (_ _ _ _ _ _ _ _ _).
Chessington World of Adventures was ace! I felt a bit scared in the %J25J2 5U2GQJ2 (_ _ _ _ _ _ _ _ _ _ _ _ _), but it was really cool! Madame #U99XU59 (_ _ _ _ _ _ _ _ _) was good too, and we went to lots of excellent MU9QUM9 (_ _ _ _ _ _ _). I liked the views from the %J25J2 QYQ (_ _ _ _ _ _ _ _ _).

2Q%9J2'9 (_ _ _ _ _ _ '_) Column in Trafalgar Square is really tall and BUCKI2GHXM *X%XCQ (_ _ _ _ _ _ _ _ _ _ _ _ _ _ _ _) is really grand—I would love to live somewhere like that! I really enjoyed seeing the Changing of the Guard Ceremony—the BX25 (_ _ _ _) and soldiers were fab! I took so many pictures at the #JWQ7 of %J25J2 (_ _ _ _ _ of _ _ _ _ _ _) and of #JWQ7 B7I5GQ (_ _ _ _ _ _ _ _ _ _ _). The city is really busy so it was nice to spend some time in HY5Q *X7K (_ _ _ _ _ _ _ _) and Regent's Park.

We got around a lot using the #UBQ (_ _ _ _). I tried a traditional roast dinner too—it was yummy! I really did love London—when can I go again?!

Can you unscramble these famous London places?

1. Hsueso fo Petlramnai

____

2. Wmisteretns Aebyb

____

3. heT Ldonno Eey

____

4. Twroe Bdregi

____

5. Bingmachuk Placae

____

6. Lnondo ooZ

____

Answers: 1. Houses of Parliament, 2. Westminster Abbey, 3. The London Eye, 4. Tower Bridge, 5. Buckingham Palace, 6. London Zoo

Summary of the trip

We had great fun, what a pity it is over ...

Whom did we meet ...

Did you meet tourists from other countries? Yes/No

If you did meet tourists, where did they come from? (Name their nationalities):

____

____

Shopping and souvenirs ...

What did you buy on the trip?

____

____

What did you want to buy, but ended up not buying?

____

____

Experiences

What are the most memorable experiences of the trip?

____

____

____

RECORD YOUR ADVENTURES!

My Journal

Date	What did we do?

ENJOY MORE FUN ADVENTURES WITH LEONARDO AND FlyingKids

ITALY

THAILAND

JAPAN

FRANCE

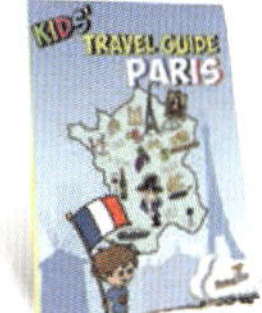

GERMANY

SPAIN

AUSTRALIA

CHINA

USA

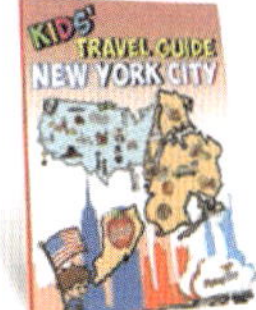

SPECIAL EDITIONS

KIDS' TRAVEL GUIDE SKI

UNITED KINGDOM

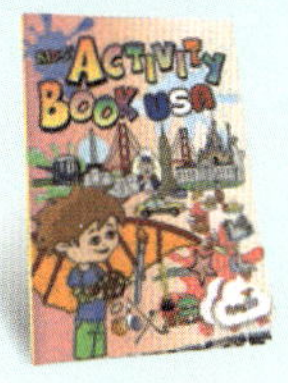

FOR FREE DOWNLOADS OF MORE ACTIVITIES, GO TO

WWW.THEFLYINGKIDS.COM

Acknowledgments

Key: t=top; b=bottom; l=left; r=right; c=center; m=main image; bg=background
All images are from Shutterstock or public domain except those mentioned.

Attributions: 25mtl-By Joel Rouse/ Ministry of Defence [see page for license], via Wikimedia Commons; 25mcr-By Ben from London, United Kingdom (Hello Great Britain) [CC BY-SA 2.0 (http://creativecommons.org/licenses/by-sa/2.0)], via Wikimedia Commons; 34mcr-By Luis Miguel Bugallo Sánchez (Lmbuga Commons)(Lmbuga Galipedia) Publicada por/Published by: Luis Miguel Bugallo Sánchez (Own work) [GFDL (http://www.gnu.org/copyleft/fdl.html) or CC-BY-SA-3.0 (http://creativecommons.org/licenses/by-sa/3.0)], via Wikimedia Commons; 43br-By Jin Zan (Own work) [CC BY-SA 3.0 (http://creativecommons.org/licenses/by-sa/3.0)], via Wikimedia Commons; 43ml-Lewis Clarke [CC BY-SA 2.0 (http://creativecommons.org/licenses/by-sa/2.0)], via Wikimedia Commons; 44m-By Sunil060902 (Own work) [CC BY-SA 3.0 (http://creativecommons.org/licenses/by-sa/3.0) or GFDL (http://www.gnu.org/copyleft/fdl.html)], via Wikimedia Commons; 47m-By Georgios Pazios (Alaniaris) (Έργο αυτού που το ανεβάζει (Own work)) [Attribution], via Wikimedia Commons; 47br-CherryX per Wikimedia Commons [CC BY-SA 3.0 (http://creativecommons.org/licenses/by-sa/3.0)], via Wikimedia Commons; 53tr-By Chris Sampson (Flickr: 310812-012 CPS) [CC BY 2.0 (http://creativecommons.org/licenses/by/2.0)], via Wikimedia Commons; 54tl-By Rob Young profile (Flickr) [CC BY 2.0 (http://creativecommons.org/licenses/by/2.0)], via Wikimedia Commons; 54bl-Alex McGregor [CC BY-SA 2.0 (http://creativecommons.org/licenses/by-sa/2.0)], via Wikimedia Commons; 55mt-By Gripweed (Own work) [CC BY-SA 3.0 (http://creativecommons.org/licenses/by-sa/3.0)], via Wikimedia Commons; 55br-www.CGPGrey.com [CC BY 3.0 (http://creativecommons.org/licenses/by/3.0)], via Wikimedia Commons; 55mb-By Duncan Harris from Nottingham, UK (London Dungeon) [CC BY 2.0 (http://creativecommons.org/licenses/by/2.0)], via Wikimedia Commons; 55tr-Photograph by Mike Peel (www.mikepeel.net) [CC BY-SA 4.0 (http://creativecommons.org/licenses/by-sa/4.0)], via Wikimedia Commons; 61mtr-DearCatastropheWaitress at en.wikipedia [GFDL (http://www.gnu.org/copyleft/fdl.html), CC-BY-SA-3.0 (http://creativecommons.org/licenses/by-sa/3.0) or CC BY 2.5 (http://creativecommons.org/licenses/by/2.5)], from Wikimedia Commons; 61mb-By Chmee2 (Own work) [CC BY-SA 3.0 (http://creativecommons.org/licenses/by-sa/3.0)], via Wikimedia Commons; 62mt-By Fæ (Self-photographed) [CC BY-SA 3.0 (http://creativecommons.org/licenses/by-sa/3.0)], via Wikimedia Commons; 62mb-PAUL FARMER [CC BY-SA 2.0 (http://creativecommons.org/licenses/by-sa/2.0)], via Wikimedia Commons; 63bl-By (ال اسور Own work) [CC BY-SA 4.0 (http://creativecommons.org/licenses/by-sa/4.0)], via Wikimedia Commons; 64mt-David Hawgood [CC BY-SA 2.0 (http://creativecommons.org/licenses/by-sa/2.0)], via Wikimedia Commons; 64bl-By Sascha Pohflepp (Flickr: V&A museum of childhood) [CC BY 2.0 (http://creativecommons.org/licenses/by/2.0)], via Wikimedia Commons; 64mb-By Scott Wylie [CC BY 2.0 (http://creativecommons.org/licenses/by/2.0)], via Wikimedia Commons; 64bl-By Cristian Bortes from Cluj-Napoca, Romania (Childhood Museum - London - September 2008) [CC BY 2.0 (http://creativecommons.org/licenses/by/2.0)], via Wikimedia Commons; 64tr-By Cristian Bortes from Cluj-Napoca, Romania (Childhood Museum - London - September 2008) [CC BY 2.0 (http://creativecommons.org/licenses/by/2.0)], via Wikimedia Commons; 65mtr-By Unicorn Theatre (Own work) [CC BY-SA 3.0 (http://creativecommons.org/licenses/by-sa/3.0)], via Wikimedia Commons; 65br-By Stmike7 (Own work) [CC BY-SA 3.0 (http://creativecommons.org/licenses/by-sa/3.0)], via Wikimedia Commons; 65mcr-Phillip Perry [CC BY-SA 2.0 (http://creativecommons.org/licenses/by-sa/2.0)], via Wikimedia Commons.